P9-BZP-869

My Secret Place

For my patient family, but
most especially for my
nephew David

First Edition 1 2 3 4 5 6 7 8 9 10
Library of Congress Cataloging in Publication Data
Magnus, Erica.   My secret place / by Erica Magnus.
p.   cm.   Summary: Describes a secret place for just one person and Bear.
ISBN 0-688-11859-3.—ISBN 0-688-11860-7 (lib. bdg.)   [1. Solitude—Fiction.
2. Bears—Fiction.] I. Title.   PZ7.M2737My   1994   [E]—dc20   93-8701   CIP   AC

My Secret Place
by Erica Magnus

Lothrop, Lee & Shepard Books New York

My secret place is just for me — and Bear.
There we eat my pinecone stew

and when we're through,
we round up cows

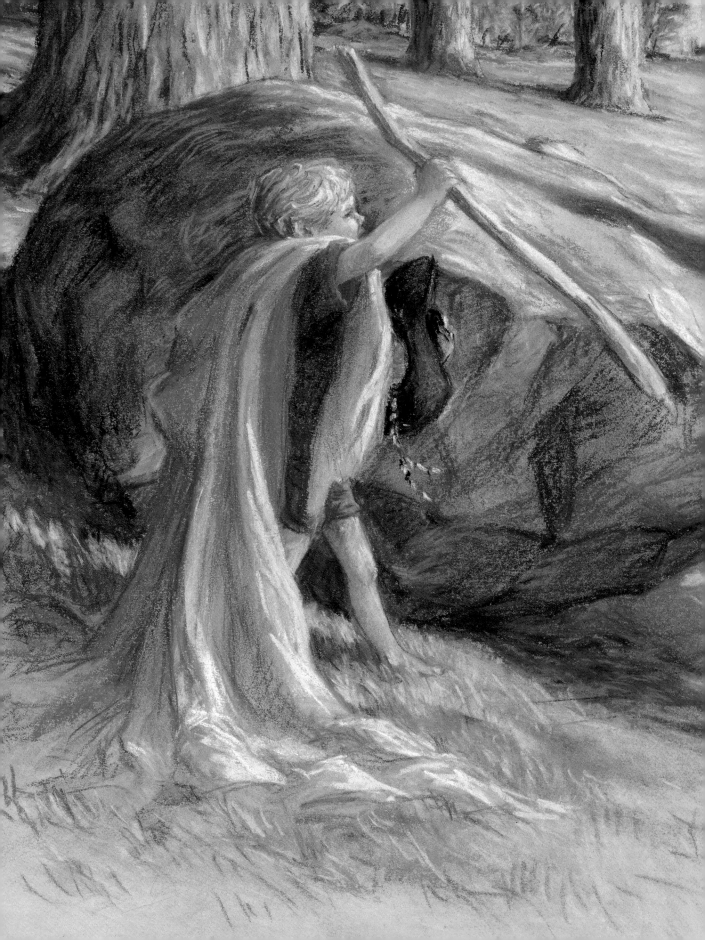

or slay a dragon.

We search for magic stones

that grow us into giants

or shrink us down to tiny ants

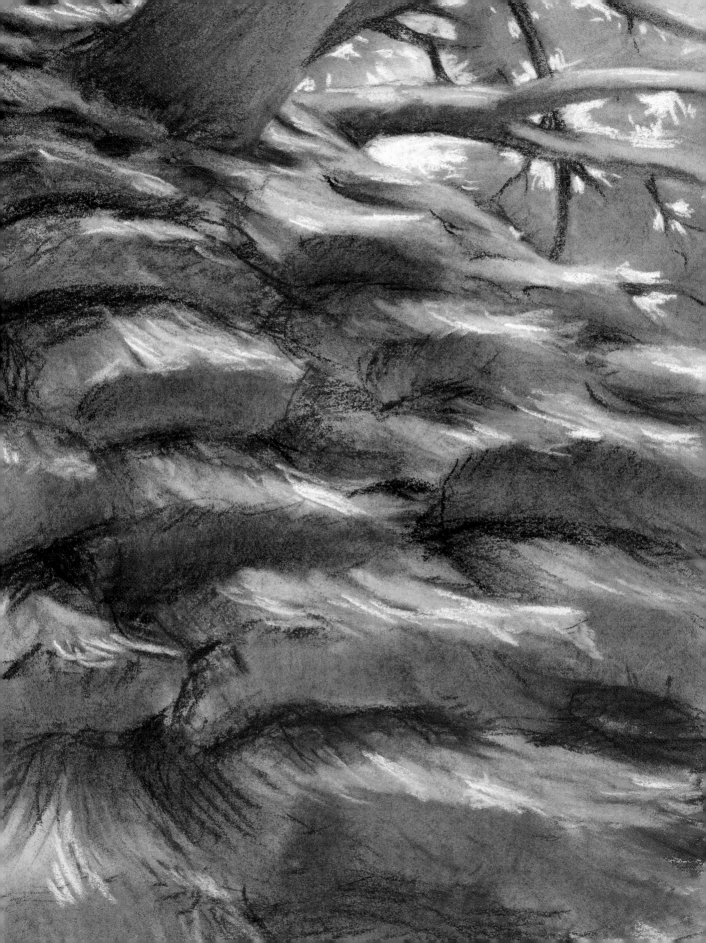

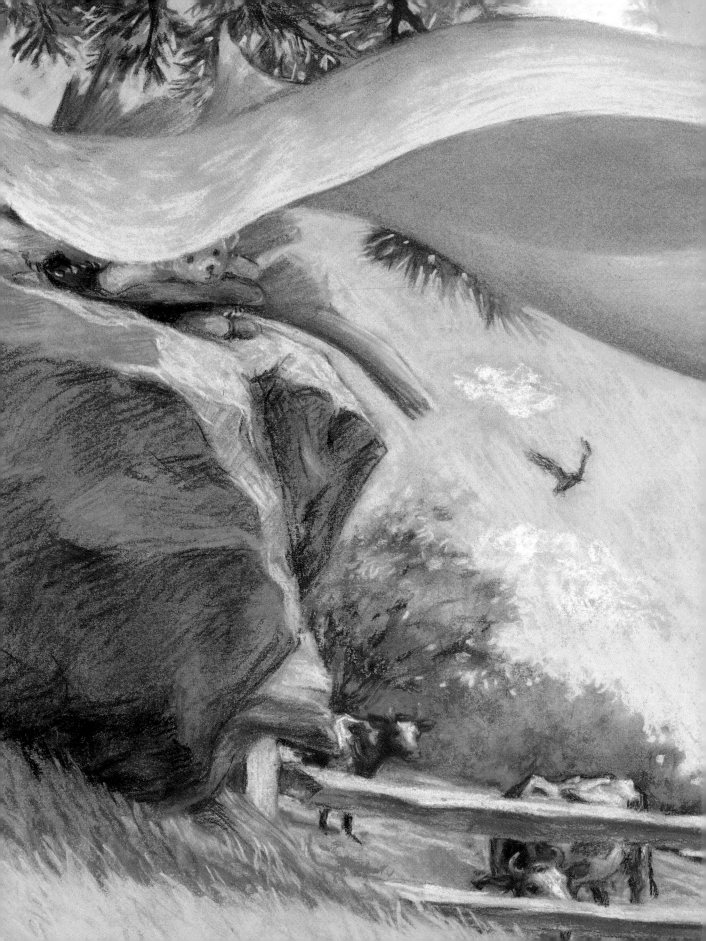

or let us fly like birds!

And if the wind turns all the leaves silver side up,
and dark clouds gather in the sky,

the rain won't find us bears

in our cozy den,

in my secret place.